Abandoned. The bus appeared
one morning from a sea of traffic –
right outside Stella's house,
where no bus should be.
Tired, old and sick,
it had a hand-painted sign on it,
held down with packing tape.

The sign said, "Heaven".

For Josephine and Alexander

First published 2011 by Walker Books Ltd, 87 Vauxhall Walk, London SE11 5HJ • © 2011 Blackbird Pty Ltd • The right of Bob Graham to be identified as author/illustrator of this work has been asserted by him in accordance with the Copyright, Designs and Patents Act 1988 • This book has been typeset in Ionic MT • Printed in China • All rights reserved. • No part of this book may be reproduced, transmitted or stored in an information retrieval system in any form or by any means, graphic, electronic or mechanical, including photocopying, taping and recording, without prior written permission from the publisher. • British Library Cataloguing in Publication Data: a catalogue record for this book is available from the British Library. • ISBN 978-1-4063-3419-7 • www.walker.co.uk • 10 9 8 7 6 5 4 3 2 1

Every one of us has the right to experience justice, fairness, freedom and truth in our lives. These important values are our human rights. Amnesty International protects people whose human rights have been taken away, and helps us all to understand our human rights better. Amnesty International has over three million members worldwide. If you would like to find out more about us and human rights education, go to www.amnesty.org.uk or www.amnesty.org.au

a bus called
heaven

BOB GRAHAM

Walker Books
AND SUBSIDIARIES
LONDON · BOSTON · SYDNEY · AUCKLAND

The bus brought change to Stella's street.
Traffic slowed where no traffic had slowed before.
People stopped and talked together – just a little, but they talked.

Stella changed, too. She took her thumb from her mouth, where it usually lived, and said, "Mummy, that old bus is sad as a whale on a beach." Then she pushed open the door and climbed on board.

Stella, the colour of moonlight,
stood among the bottles, cans and rubbish.

She was so pale you could
almost see through her.
"It could be ... ours," she whispered.

"Whose?" asked Nicky, Vicky, Alex, Yasmin and Po.
"What did she say?" asked Mrs Dimitros.

"Ours!"
she said louder.

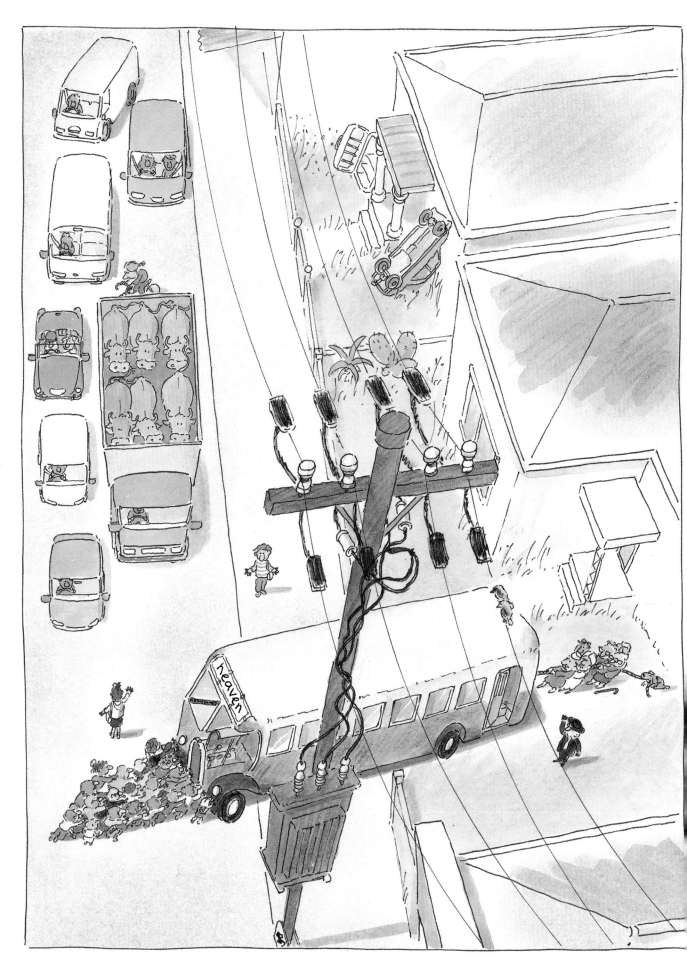

"Well, whoever's it is, it needs to come off the road," said Stella's mum ...

and when Dad came home that afternoon, he found an old bus where the front garden used to be. "The wheels stick out on the pavement," he said. "There are sure to be regulations…"

"Well, it's staying here," said Stella.
"That's my regulation."

Next morning, Stella looked out of her front window.
People sat on the wall, where no one had sat before.

Under the bus were Esther, Rajit, Chelsea and Charles.
"Mummy," said Stella, "I'm going out." And she joined them.

That day, the bus settled in.
Weeds nudged up around
the tyres. Snails made
silver trails, and a pair of
sparrows nested in the
old engine.

While the children played, the grown-ups
mopped and scrubbed and polished.

That night, the bus saw a bit of new paint.

"Hello, boys!" said Mum. "I've got an idea! Come back tomorrow –
and you can paint the whole bus. Make it sparkle."

Next morning, Stella drew a picture for the Ratz to copy.

People came with donations for the old bus.

Popi brought her goldfish, Eric.

Luke gave a set of Supercomix.

Stella carried in her table football with the goalie missing.

Mrs Stavros brought a bus cake.

And Lucy lent her dog, Bear – for anyone who needed to just sit and pat something.

Life returned to the old bus.
Stella's fingers fluttered and her footballers spun.

Babies crawled,

people laughed,

kids fought,

grandads scratched dogs,

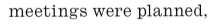

meetings were planned,

couples met

and the Fingles showed their holiday pictures.

One Saturday morning,
just outside Stella's house,
there was music and dancing,
there were picnics and laughter ...

when a tow truck arrived.

"It's against regulations!" said the driver.
"This bus is causing an obstruction."

"He means it sticks out," Stella's dad
whispered.

"The bus has to go,"

said the driver.

As the front wheels left the ground,
snails dropped from under the bus
and a twittering came from
the old engine.

"Go where?"

gasped the crowd.

"To the BONEYARD,"

came the reply.

The crowd pleaded for their bus, but the Boneyard Boss
came out to join the driver and shook his head.

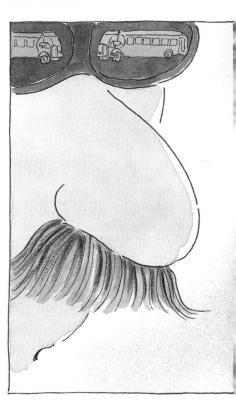

"This one's for the CRUSHER!"

A little pink glow crept across Stella's cheek. Three rescued snails were deep in her pocket. "Excuse me," she said. "Shall we play table football?

"You can have the only goalie ... but if I win, we'll keep the bus."

"And why," asked the Boneyard Boss, "tell me why
should I play you for the bus?"

"Because," replied Stella, "there are sparrows nesting in the engine."

The game began. Handles spun. The ball smacked end to end, then ...

GOAL!

Stella scored.

She followed that with nine more – and won!
The boss put out his hand. "Joe," he said.
"Stella," said Stella – and shook it.

Then Stella ran to
the front of the bus.

"Come and see," she said...

"Chicks!"

Amid the frantic flapping of the parent sparrows'
wings, Joe the Boneyard Boss spoke quietly.
"Better get your bus to somewhere safe, kid.
Somewhere out of the way."

"Thank you!" said Stella.

And the crowd cheered.

"I know where we can take it!" said Stella.

While the others pushed, she and Mum sat up front to steer ...

almost back to where they'd started from.

And when the old bus came to rest at last, everyone else needed a rest too. Well, *almost* everyone...

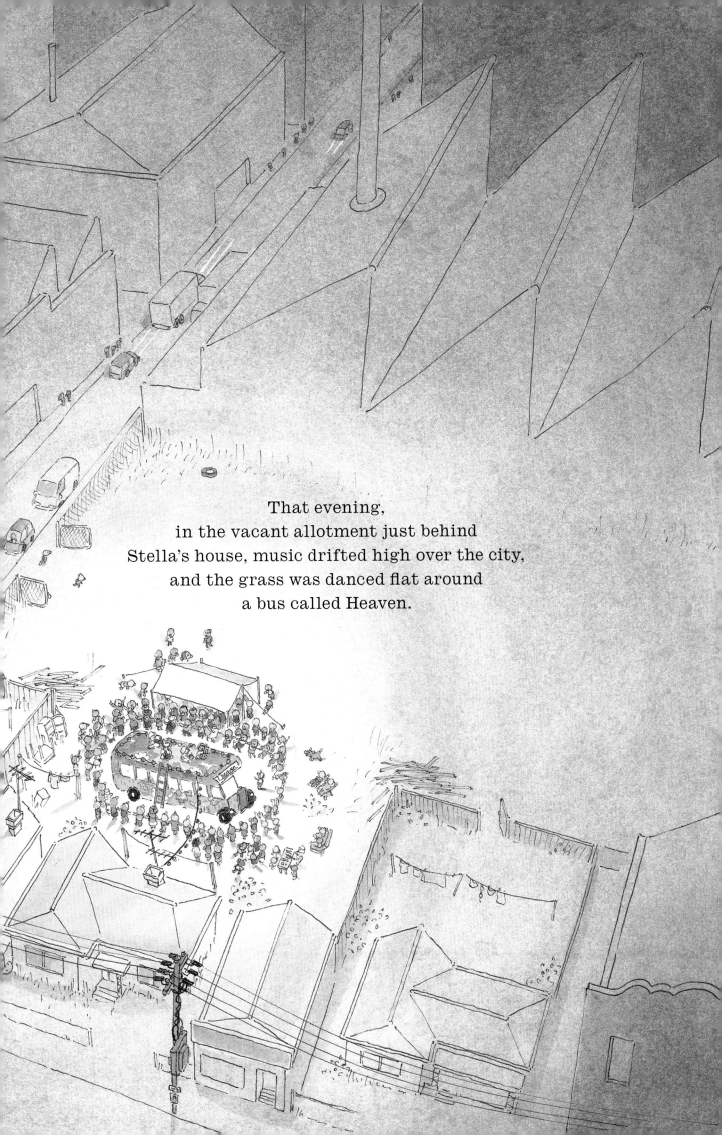

That evening,
in the vacant allotment just behind
Stella's house, music drifted high over the city,
and the grass was danced flat around
a bus called Heaven.

As a full moon rose,
three snails slid safely back
under the tyres.

And tomorrow, Stella will see
the sparrow chicks fly
for the first time.